Thank you Fräulein Gasterstädt

Thank you Lane Smith

Thank you Stinky Cheese Man

Before this book

I wrote another book and called it *10 (ten)*.

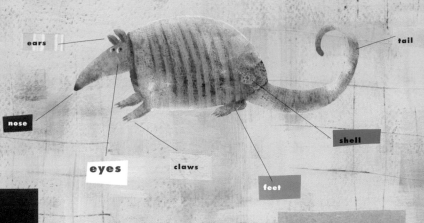

The Armadillo
(naked, after taking a bath)

ears

tail

nose

shell

eyes

claws

feet

(ten)

10

First,
they put on nice ear socks. Always clean. Always in bright colors.

Second,
a well brought up armadillo never leaves home without a proper tail stocking.

Third,
they always, always paint their noses, usually blue (nobody knows why).

Fourth,
they always wear pretty dresses or elegant suits.

Fifth,
armadillos usually walk on all four legs, but sometimes they walk on two, like you and me. It all depends on their mood. Most of the time they are in a very good mood.

It was all about armadillos. What they wear and why, and what their names are (their names are Mr. and Mrs. Armadillo),

and where they live,

and how Mrs. Armadillo got very fat, but really she wasn't just fat, she was having a baby, and Mr. Armadillo was so worried and took her to the hospital in the middle of the night,

and who was born and how many and what their names are (their names are One, Two, Three, Four, Five, Six, Seven, Eight, Nine, and Ten).

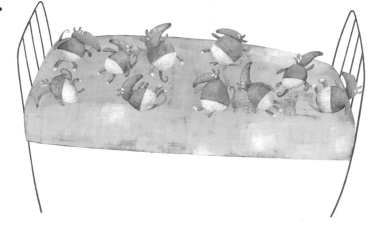

Now look at that pink one, the one that looks like a piglet. My new story is about him.

(one)

#

A nice story about an awful braggart

by V. Radunsky

Viking

One

Two

Three

Four (just his tail and hind paws—he's shy)

Five

1 2 3 4 5

Here they are, all 10 little armadillos in one bathtub.
Look carefully at that pink one.

His name is Six.

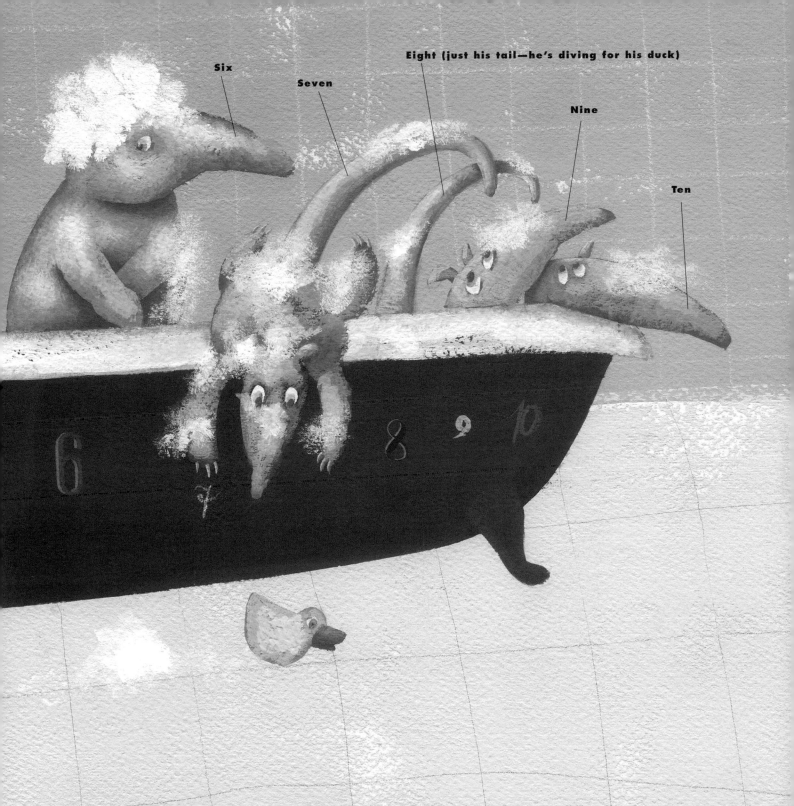

Six

Seven

Eight (just his tail—he's diving for his duck)

Nine

Ten

His parents named him Six.

His grandma and grandpa call him Six.

His uncle and aunt call him Six.

His brothers and sisters call him Six.

But he says he is #1.

Grandma Armadillo   Mrs. Armadillo (Mother)   Mr. Armadillo (Father)

It all started just the other day when we heard Six say:

I'm #1. I'm the best. I'm #1. I am #1!"

Everybody heard it: Grandma Armadillo, Mrs. Armadillo (mother), Mr. Armadillo (father), Grandpa Armadillo, Uncle Elmer and his wife (both armadillos), and all the armadillo children. Even the dog heard it.

I'm the best. I am #1!"

Grandpa Armadillo,
who is crazy about baseball

Uncle Elmer's wife,
who loves animals

Uncle Elmer,
who wanted to be a ballerina

And then he said:

"Have you noticed that I am incredibly tall for my age?

I'm the tallest!"

And he said:

"I am so smart that I am going to college tomorrow. I've already read a billion books. And I'm just five.

I'm the smartest!"

And:

"I invented a secret formula for growing hair. You see, you are all bald now [it's true, armadillos don't have hair], but soon you will look like this. You will be nice and warm.

I'm th #1 inv ntor!"

I am the fastest.

I'm like Super Jet.

Hey, what was that? Was that me? Wow, that WAS fast!

My dog is the biggest! **We are #1!**

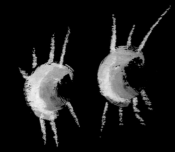

I'm the bravest!

I'm not afraid of the dark.

I'm not even afraid to scream in the dark.

A a a

a

a a a

a a

a

a

a

a

a

a

a

a

ah!

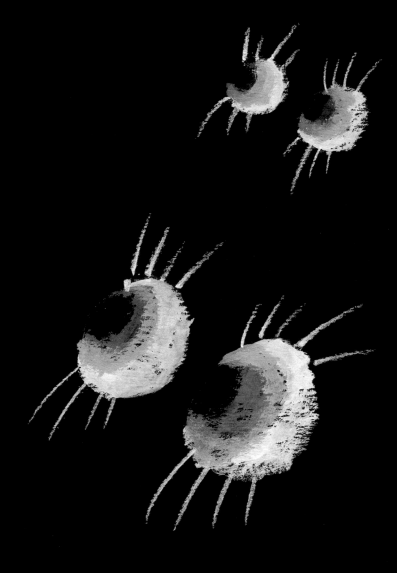

Were you scared?
I bet you were scared!

I'm the strongest!

I saved this horse from drowning the other day.
Twenty grown armadillos couldn't even lift this horse,
but I did. Because I'm #1. The horse was so grateful.

I have more best friends than anybody!

I'm friends with Madeline, Pinocchio, Maisy, and Winnie-the-Pooh.
The Stinky Cheese Man is my #1 best friend.
Just the other day, I bumped into him on the street.
"Hi Stinky," I said. "How are you?" And you know what he
said to me? He said, "I'm fine."

I'm #1 in my family!

For my birthday, I will get all the presents I want.

What do I want? I want:

1. Three cats plus one more cat. Five altogether.

2. A red bicycle, maybe even two.

3. A signed photo of Pinocchio.

4. A Superman outfit.

5. Black stick-on fingernails, really scary.

6. Sunglasses like those spies in the movies.

That's all I want.

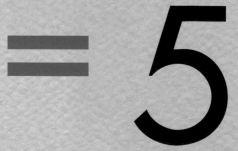

Look, look! Look what I built!
Can't you see? It's a racing car.
I'm a racer.

I'm the #1 racer!

I am #1,

I am #1,

am #1!

Here everybody started talking at once.

Mrs. Armadillo said,

"Yes. You are #1."

And Mr. Armadillo said,

"You are the best."

And Uncle Elmer and his wife (also armadillos) said,

"Oh, yes. #1."

And Grandma and Grandpa Armadillo both said,

#1

"#1. Definitely."

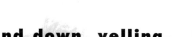

And all the armadillo children were jumping up and down, yelling,

#1

You are the #1 clown, show-off, chatterbox, storyteller, dreamer!

You are our

#1

VIKING Published by Penguin Group
Penguin Young Readers Group, 345 Hudson Street, New York, New York 10014, U.S.A.

First published in 2003 by Viking, a division of Penguin Young Readers Group

10   9   8   7   6   5   4   3   2   1

LIBRARY OF CONGRESS CATALOGING-IN-PUBLICATION DATA   Radunsky, Vladimir.   One / by Vladimir Radunsky.   p. cm.   Sequel to: Ten.
Summary: When Six, a pink armadillo with nine green siblings, brags that he is "#1" in everything, his family expresses a different
opinion.   ISBN 0-670-03564-5 (hardcover)   [1. Pride and vanity—Fiction. 2. Armadillos—Fiction.] I. Title.
PZ7.R1226On 2003   [E]—dc21   2003005790   Manufactured in China.